Zoom! Zoom! Zoom! I'm Off to the Moon!

dan yaccarino

SCHOLASTIC PRESS   NEW YORK

Zoom! Zoom! Zoom! I'm off to the moon.

All rights reserved. Published by Scholastic Press, a division of Scholastic Inc., PUBLISHERS SINCE 1920. SCHOLASTIC and SCHOLASTIC PRESS and associated logos are trademarks and/or registered trademarks of Scholastic Inc.

No part of this publication may be reproduced, or stored in a retrieval system, or transmitted in any form or by any means, electronic, mechanical, photocopying, recording, or otherwise, without written permission of the publisher. For information regarding permission, write to Scholastic Inc., Attention: Permissions Department, 555 Broadway, New York, NY 10012.

LIBRARY OF CONGRESS CATALOGING-IN-PUBLICATION DATA
Yaccarino, Dan.
Zoom! Zoom! Zoom! I'm off to the moon / Dan Yaccarino. — 1st ed.
p. cm.
Summary: A boy gets in a spaceship and takes a dangerous but exciting trip to the moon.
ISBN 0-590-95610-8
[1. Space flight to the moon—Fiction. 2. Moon—Exploration—Fiction. 3. Stories in rhyme.] I. Title
PZ8.3.Y24Zo   1997
[E]—dc21   96-52705
CIP AC
4 6 8 10 9 7 5
Printed in the U.S.A.   36
First edition, September 1997

The illustrations are alkyds on watercolor paper.
The type was set in Bernhard Gothic Ultra.
Design by Kristina Iulo

Up, up, and away,
I'm leaving today.

First, space suit,

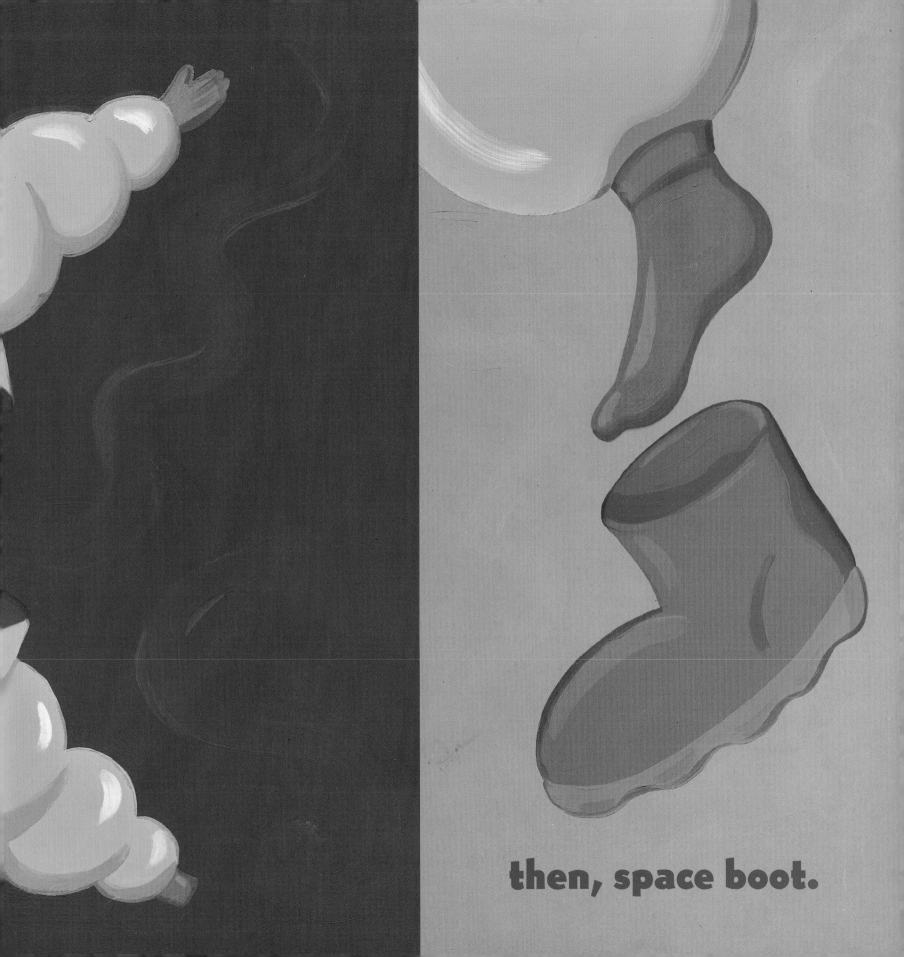

then, space boot.

Strapped inside,

0 - 1 - 2

Countdown counting...
Excitement mounting...

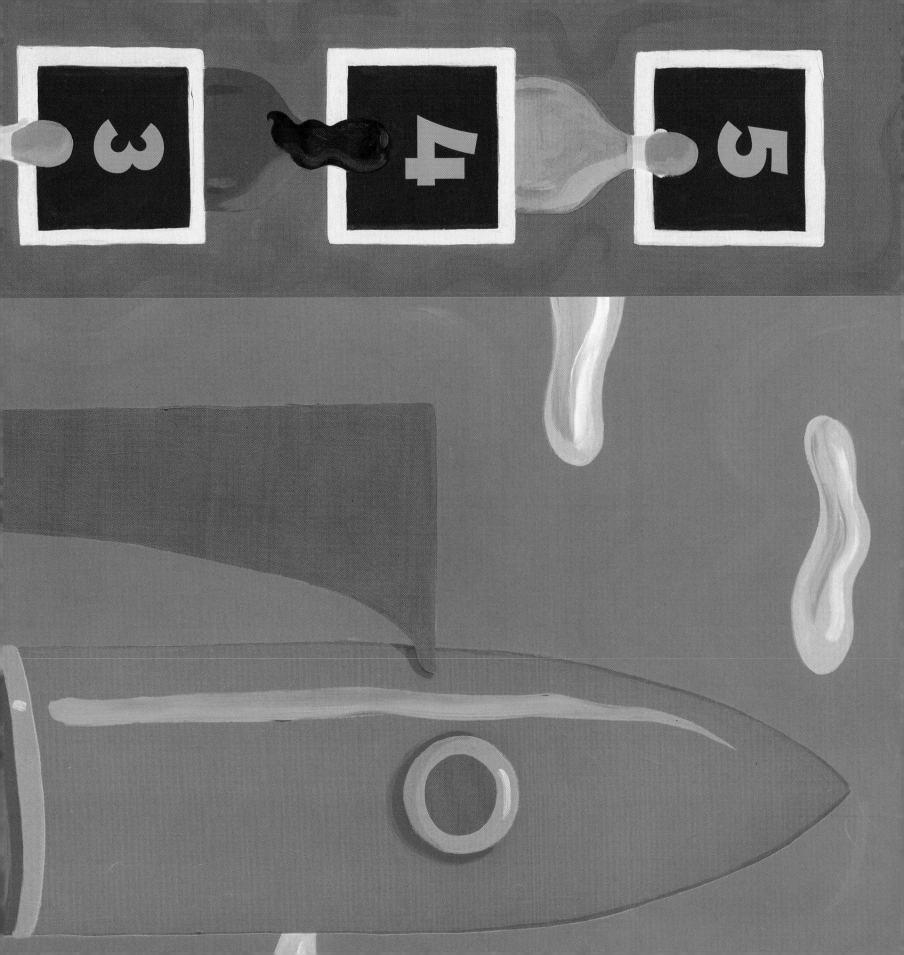

Boosters blast!
Moving fast.
Engines roaring.
Rocket soaring.

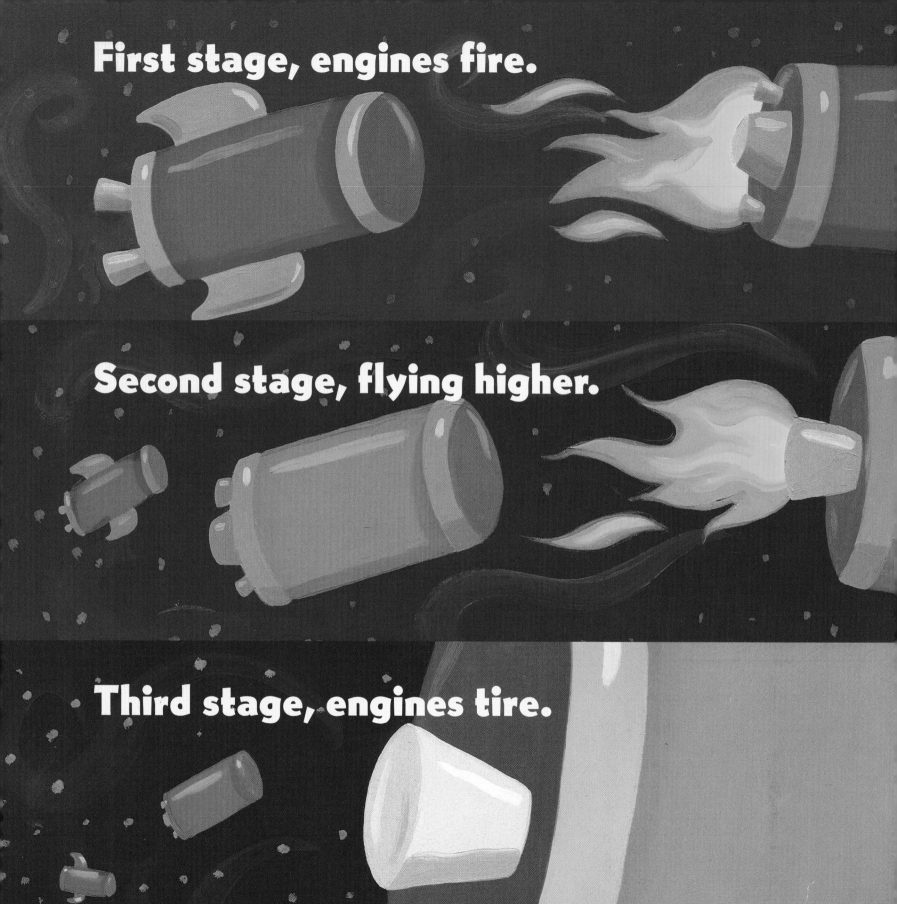

First stage, engines fire.

Second stage, flying higher.

Third stage, engines tire.

There's outer space all over the place.

Floating around without a sound.

Just avoid the asteroids.

Lunar rover,
driving over.

Moon rocks in a box.

Dark skies.

Earthrise.

Comets fly.
Now say...

...Good-bye.

LIGHTS WINKING.

PANELS

BLINKING.

BUTTONS
AND
DIALS

COUNT THE MILES.

A sonic boom. I'm landing soon.

SPLASH DOWN! Safe and sound.

Across the nation —

...from the moon.